CORDUROY
Writes a Letter

Story by **Alison Inches**

Illustrations by **Allan Eitzen**

Based on the characters created by
Don Freeman

PUFFIN BOOKS

PUFFIN BOOKS
Published by Penguin Group
Penguin Young Readers Group,
345 Hudson Street, New York, New York 10014, U.S.A.
Penguin Books Ltd, 80 Strand, London WC2R ORL, England
Penguin Books Australia Ltd, 250 Camberwell Road, Camberwell, Victoria 3124, Australia
Penguin Books Canada Ltd, 10 Alcorn Avenue, Toronto, Ontario, Canada M4V 3B2
Penguin Books (N.Z.) Ltd, 182-190 Wairau Road, Auckland 10, New Zealand

First published in the United States of America by Viking,
a division of Penguin Putnam Books for Young Readers, 2002
Published by Puffin Books, a division of Penguin Young Readers Group, 2004

1   3   5   7   9   10   8   6   4   2

Copyright © Penguin Putnam Inc., 2002
Text by Alison Inches
Illustrations by Allan Eitzen
All rights reserved

THE LIBRARY OF CONGRESS HAS CATALOGED THE VIKING EDITION AS FOLLOWS:
Inches, Alison.
Corduroy writes a letter / by Alison Inches ; illustrated by Allan Eitzen;
p. cm.
Based on a character created by Don Freeman.
Summary: Corduroy shows Lisa that writing letters to express your opinion can make a difference.
ISBN: 0-670-03548-3 (hc)
[1. Letter writing—Fiction. 2. Letters—Fiction. 3. Teddy bears—Fiction.]
I. Eitzen, Allan, ill.   II. Freeman, Don, 1908–1978.   III. Title.
PZ7.1355 Cmk   2002   [E]—dc21   2002006154

Puffin Easy-to-Read ISBN 0-14-240130-7
Puffin® and Easy-to-Read® are registered trademarks of Penguin Group (USA) Inc.

Manufactured in China
Set in Bookman

Reading Level 1.8

CORDUROY
Writes a Letter

Lisa took a big bite of her cookie.

"*Hmmm*," she said.

"Something's different. I know what it is.
It doesn't have enough sprinkles!"

"Why don't you write the bakery a letter?"
said her mother.

"Tell them the cookies need
more sprinkles."

"Good idea!" said Lisa.

She got out a pen

and a pad of paper.

She stared at the pad.

The clock went

Tick tick.

Tick tick.

After a while, she said,

"What's the use, Corduroy?

The bakery owner will not listen to me.

I'm just a little girl."

She put down her pen and left.

Maybe I can write a letter, thought Corduroy.

He wrote:

Dear Mr. Bakery Owner:

We love your cookies.

We buy them every Saturday.

Today there were fewer sprinkles.

We thought you should know.

Yours sincerely,

Corduroy

Corduroy put the letter in an envelope

and mailed it.

The next Saturday, Lisa and Corduroy
picked up the cookies.

"Look, Corduroy!" said Lisa.

"The cookies have more sprinkles!"

"That's right!" said the owner.

"Someone sent me a letter."

THEATER

That night, Lisa and her mother went
to the movies.

Corduroy went, too.

"Hey, look at the sign!" said Lisa.

"The lights are out on two of the letters.

The sign says MOVIE EATER.

It should say MOVIE THEATER."

Lisa and her mother laughed.

"Why don't you write the owner a letter?"
said her mother.

"Maybe I will," said Lisa.

After the movie, Lisa got a pen and a pad of paper.

"What should I write, Corduroy?" said Lisa.

She thought and thought.

Soon Lisa began to feel sleepy.

"It's no use," said Lisa.

"The movie theater owner is too important.

He will not read a letter from me."

She went to bed.

But Corduroy was not ready for bed.

I can write a letter, thought Corduroy.

Corduroy got the pen and pad.

He sat under the night-light and wrote:

Dear Mr. Movie Theater Owner:

Last night, we went to your theater.

We noticed your sign.

Two of your lights are out.

Yours truly,

Corduroy

On Thursday, Lisa and her mother
walked past the movie theater.

THEATER

Lisa looked at the sign.

"It's all fixed!" she said.

"That's neat," said Lisa.

"The next time I have something to say,

I'm going to write a letter."

Every day, Lisa listened to music on the radio.

Corduroy listened, too.

"I love this new radio station," said Lisa.

"But I wish they would play 'Teddy Bear Bop.'

That's my favorite song.

"I should write the station

and ask them to play it," said Lisa.

Great idea! thought Corduroy.

Lisa got her pen and pad.

She wrote:

Dear WROC:

I listen to your station every day.

I wish you would play "Teddy Bear Bop."

It's my favorite song.

It's my bear Corduroy's favorite song, too.

Thanks for being the best station ever.

Yours truly,

Lisa

Lisa put the letter into an envelope
and mailed it.

The following week,

Lisa had the radio on.

The deejay said,

"This next song is for Corduroy

from Lisa."

Then "Teddy Bear Bop" began to play.

Lisa and Corduroy danced around

the room.

"Wow!" said Lisa.

"They're playing our song!"

See, thought Corduroy.

It pays to write letters!